Seals

Thea Feldman

First published 2015 by Kingfisher
an imprint of Macmillan Children's Books
20 New Wharf Road, London N1 9RR
Associated companies throughout the world
www.panmacmillan.com

Series editor: Polly Goodman
Literacy consultant: Hilary Horton

ISBN 978-0-7534-3909-8

9 8 7 6 5 4 3 2 1

1TR/0615/WKT/UG/105MA

A CIP catalogue record for this book is available from the British Library.

Printed in China

Picture credits
The Publisher would like to thank the following for permission to reproduce their material.
Top = t; Bottom = b; Centre = c; Left = l; Right = r
Cover Shutterstock/Bildagentur Zoonar GmbH; Pages 3 Naturepl/Bryan & Cherry Alexander;
4–5 FLPA/Minden Pictures/Norbert Wu; 6 Alamy/Wolfgang Polzer; 7 Alamy/tbkmedia.de;
8 Shutterstock/Randimal; 9 FLPA/Samuel Blanc/Biosphoto; 10 Shutterstock/David Osborn;
11 Alamy/Andrey Nekrasov; 12 Getty/David Fleetham/Visuals Unlimited Inc., 13t Shutterstock/
CVancoillie; 13b FLPA/Imagebroker/Norbert Probst; 14 Alamy/Nature Picture Library; 15 Naturepl/
Doug Perrine; 16 Shutterstock/Volt Collection; 17 Shutterstock/duchy; 18–19 Alamy/Robert Harding
World Imagery; 20–21 Alamy/Steve Bloom Images; 22–23 Shutterstock/phodo; 24 Shutterstock/
bikeriderlondon; 25 Shutterstock/David Osborn; 26 Alamy/James Beards; 27 Alamy/imageBROKER;
28 Shutterstock/Steve Photography; 29 Alamy/imageBROKER; 30–31 Shutterstock/Stefan Simmerl.

Splash!

A seal dives into the water.

This seal can dive down as deep as 200 metres.

It can hold its breath
for about 20 minutes!

How long can you hold
your breath?

A seal dives to look for food.

Seals eat fish,
shrimps, squid and
other sea creatures.

There are many different kinds of seal.

Some seals have spots.

Some seals have white bands.

The elephant seal is the biggest seal of all.

The ringed seal is one
of the smallest seals.

Look at the body of this seal.

It is thick in the middle
and thinner at each end.

This shape helps the seal to
move easily through water.

A seal has **flippers** instead of hands and feet!

Flippers help a seal to move well in the water.

A seal can sleep in the water.

Some seals can even sleep under the water!

The holes in its **nostrils** close when a seal is under the water.

Most seals live in the sea.

These seals live in a **lake**.

Many seals live in cold places.

Some of them have thick
fur that helps to keep their
body warm.

These seals are called fur seals.

Other seals have **blubber**
to help keep them warm.

Blubber is a thick layer
of fat under the skin.

Sometimes seals come out of the water and stay on land.

It is hard for seals to
move around on land.

Fur seals push themselves
forwards with all four flippers.

This seal is sliding
on its tummy!

Why do seals come out of the water onto land?

They come to **mate** and have baby seals.

A male seal is called a **bull**.

A female seal is called a **cow**.

Sometimes bulls fight other bulls.

A baby seal is called a **pup**.
A cow has one pup at a time.

A mother seal
leaves her pup when
it is two weeks old.

The pup stays on land for
a few more weeks.

Then it is ready to swim.

Splash!

Glossary

blubber the fat under the skin of a seal

bull a daddy seal

cow a mummy seal

flippers the hands and feet of a seal

lake a large area of water surrounded by land

mate to find a partner to have babies with

nostrils the holes in a seal's nose for breathing

pup a baby seal